We Are Brothers

Written by Da-yun Oh

Illustrated by Anna Godeassi

Edited by Joy Cowley

I was playing with my little brother.
We were playing a game with robots.
My robot was old. His robot was new.
"Yee-hah!" we yelled. *Bang, bang, bang!*

Dad shouted at us, "Quiet, boys!
Go to your room!"

I said to my little brother,
"Let's change robots."

He hid his robot behind his back.

"I just want to play with yours one time,"
I said, reaching for his new toy.

He yelled, "Dad! Dad!
He's trying to take my robot!"

Dad came in, angry with me.
"You go and sit in the thinking chair!"

Dad doesn't know anything.
I just wanted to play
with the new toy.

6

I would be very happy
if I lived in a house full of toys.
Everything would be mine!
Every day would be like my birthday.

I decided to ignore my brother.
I stared at the TV, but he began to giggle.

I tried to get the remote
so I could change the channel.

"No!" he said. "I want to watch this!"
He sat on the remote
and stuck his tongue out at me.

When I pushed him away
and grabbed the remote,
he started to cry.

Mum rushed in,
and my little brother ran to her.
He was crying loudly.
Mum said to me,
"You are the big brother.
Why did you hit him?"

"I didn't hit him!" I said.
"I just pushed him."

But Mum said, "You go and sit
in the thinking chair."

Mum doesn't know anything.
She doesn't know how angry
I am to be the big brother.

12

If I was a clear jellyfish,
no one would see me.
I would eat my brother's ice cream.
I would push him and poke him.
No one would know
I was his big brother.

Dinner time was a silent battle.
I stared at my little brother.
He stared back at me.
I pushed his chair.
He pushed my chair.
When I touched his dish,
he touched my dish.
Tap, tap, tap-tap-tap!

I stood up and shouted at him.
"You are such a jerk!"

Mum and Dad got mad at me.
"What's wrong with you today?"

"Why do you always blame me?" I yelled.
"You don't know anything!"

So here I am, in the thinking chair.
I'm the one who always gets punished.
I'd like to go away and be anywhere but here.

18

I wish I could fly like a bird in this chair.
I'd fly so high in my chair that
I would not be able to see my house.
I would not be able to see my little brother.

But then I hear my brother
calling me. He is saying,
"Why are you on that chair
all by yourself?"

I stop dreaming.
My little brother has a dining chair.
He is pulling it over beside me.
"What are you doing?" I ask.

"I want to be with you," he says.

He and I have a late dinner.
"Did you cry?" he asks.

"No," I say.

"You did so," he says.

"I did not!"

"Yes, you did! You did!"

And, so we are at it again!

Dear Little Brother,

I'm sorry for calling you names.
We were having fun playing with robots together,
and then it turned into a big fight. I'm not sure how that happened.

Sometimes it feels like Mum and Dad take your side and that they
love you more. That is why I get mad at you sometimes, even though
I really like you.

If anyone else ever picked on you, I would run to protect you and help you.
We are a team. But when we are at home with Mum and Dad, sometimes
I feel like you are my enemy. We compete with each other to get toys
or the TV remote or attention from Mum and Dad.

But even then, we are still brothers. You will always be my baby brother,
and I will always be your big brother.
I will always love you!

With love.
from your big brother

big & SMALL

Original Korean text by Da-yun Oh
Illustrations by Anna Godeassi
Original Korean edition © Eenbook 2011

This English edition published by Big & Small in 2015
by arrangement with Eenbook
English text edited by Joy Cowley
Additional editing by Mary Lindeen
Artwork for this edition produced
in cooperation with Norwood House Press, USA
English edition © Big & Small 2015

ISBN: 978-1-925234-01-5

Printed in Korea